To Harry's family and mine—Lisa, Kate, and James
—M. G.

For Peter and Mathew, who are the bestest
—S. M.

Henry Holt and Company, LLC, *Publishers since 1866*
115 West 18th Street, New York, New York 10011
www.henryholt.com

Henry Holt is a registered trademark of Henry Holt and Company, LLC
Text copyright © 2003 by Mark Gibbel. Illustrations copyright © 2003 by Sarah Massini.
All rights reserved. Distributed in Canada by H. B. Fenn and Company Ltd.

Library of Congress Cataloging-in-Publication Data
Gibbel, Mark. Oh, Harry! / Mark Gibbel; illustrated by Sarah Massini.
Summary: On his first night with his new family, Harry the kitten tries sleeping in every bed but his own.
[1. Cats—Fiction. 2. Pets—Fiction.] I. Massini, Sarah, ill. II. Title. PZ7.G339096Oh 2003   [E]—dc21   2002012840

ISBN 0-8050-6851-1 / First Edition—2003 / Designed and hand-lettered by Sarah Massini
Printed in the United States of America on acid-free paper. ∞
1 3 5 7 9 10 8 6 4 2

The artist used a combination of ink, charcoal, watercolor, acrylic, and
colored pencil to create the illustrations for this book.

Author royalties from Oh, Harry! will benefit Project Reach Youth of Brooklyn, New York,
a community organization that serves more than 7,000 young people and their families.

Oh, Harry!

written by **Mark** Gibbel

illustrated by **Sarah** **Massini**

Henry Holt and Company

NEW YORK

Good night, Harry.

Oh, Harry!

Oh, Harry!